Dear Parents:

Congratulations! Your child is taking the first steps on an exciting journey. The destination? Independent reading!

STEP INTO READING® will help your child get there. The program offers five steps to reading success. Each step includes fun stories and colorful art or photographs. In addition to original fiction and books with favorite characters, there are Step into Reading Non-Fiction Readers, Phonics Readers and Boxed Sets, Sticker Readers, and Comic Readers—a complete literacy program with something to interest every child.

Learning to Read, Step by Step!

Ready to Read   Preschool–Kindergarten
• big type and easy words • rhyme and rhythm • picture clues
For children who know the alphabet and are eager to begin reading.

Reading with Help   Preschool–Grade 1
• basic vocabulary • short sentences • simple stories
For children who recognize familiar words and sound out new words with help.

Reading on Your Own   Grades 1–3
• engaging characters • easy-to-follow plots • popular topics
For children who are ready to read on their own.

Reading Paragraphs   Grades 2–3
• challenging vocabulary • short paragraphs • exciting stories
For newly independent readers who read simple sentences with confidence.

Ready for Chapters   Grades 2–4
• chapters • longer paragraphs • full-color art
For children who want to take the plunge into chapter books but still like colorful pictures.

STEP INTO READING® is designed to give every child a successful reading experience. The grade levels are only guides; children will progress through the steps at their own speed, developing confidence in their reading.

Remember, a lifetime love of reading starts with a single step!

For Melissa —A.J.

Published in the United States by Random House Children's Books, a division of Penguin Random House LLC, 1745 Broadway, New York, NY 10019, and in Canada by Random House of Canada, a division of Penguin Random House Ltd., Toronto.

Step into Reading, Random House, and the Random House colophon are registered trademarks of Penguin Random House LLC.

Visit us on the Web!
StepIntoReading.com
randomhousekids.com

Educators and librarians, for a variety of teaching tools, visit us at RHTeachersLibrarians.com

ISBN 978-1-101-93245-2 (trade) — ISBN 978-1-101-93246-9 (lib. bdg.) —
ISBN 978-1-101-93247-6 (ebook)

Printed in the United States of America

10 9 8 7 6 5 4 3 2 1

Barbie™

I Can Be a Farm Vet

By Apple Jordan

Illustrated by Kellee Riley

Random House 🏠 New York

Barbie visits
her friend Emma.
Emma is a farm vet.

Barbie wants
to be a farm vet,
too!

Today is a busy day.
Emma and Barbie
are going
to visit the animals
on Sunshine Farm.

They drive to the farm
in Emma's truck.

First, Emma checks
on a calf.
He was born last night.
A heat lamp
keeps him warm.

Today he is trying
to stand.

The mother cow
is resting.

Emma brings her hay.

Barbie brings her water.

A sheep is sick.

Emma gives the sheep
some medicine.

A young horse
has a sore leg.

Emma wraps
the foal's leg
with a bandage.

Emma and Barbie
check a pig
and her piglets.

They make sure
the pigs are eating well.
Each one is healthy!

Goats' hooves must be
cleaned and trimmed.

Emma shows Barbie
and the farmer how
to trim a goat's hoof.

Next, they check
on the chickens
in the chicken coop.

Emma makes sure
they are healthy
to lay their eggs.

A farm vet takes care
of llamas, too.

Emma listens
to a llama's heart.
The llamas
are all healthy.

Emma is
a great farm vet.
Someday Barbie
will be a vet, too!